ALL CHALKED UP

CARTOON NETWORK™

by Amy Keating Rogers

SCHOLASTIC INC.

New York   Toronto   London   Auckland   Sydney
Mexico City   New Delhi   Hong Kong

ISBN 0-439-16020-0

Cover design by Peter Koblish • Interior design by Kay Petronio

12 11 10 9 8 7 6 5 4 3 2 1   0 1 2 3 4 5/0

Printed in the United States
First Scholastic printing, March 2000

SUGAR . . .

SPICE . . .

and everything nice . . .

These were the ingredients chosen to

create the perfect little girls.

But Professor Utonium accidentally

added an extra ingredient to

the concoction —

CHEMICAL X!

And thus, the Powerpuff Girls were born!

Using their ultra superpowers

BLOSSOM,

BUBBLES,

and **BUTTERCUP**

have dedicated their lives to fighting crime

and the forces of evil!

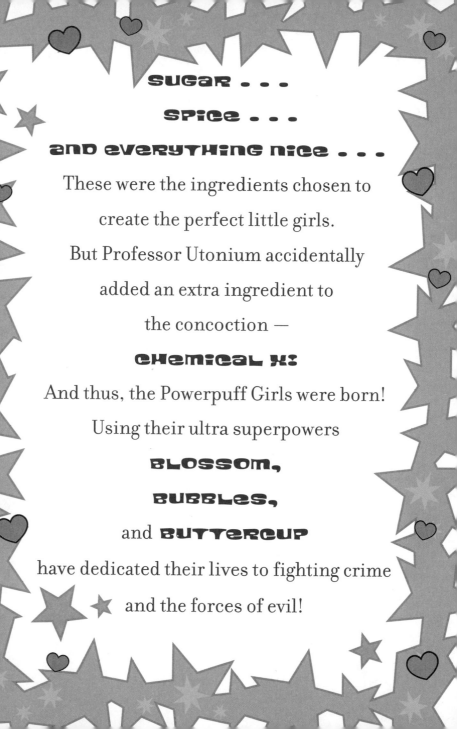

chapter 1

The city of Townsville. Our story begins at the home of the Powerpuff Girls.

That morning, the Girls — Blossom, Bubbles, and Buttercup — were in their room, getting ready for school. As usual, it was a peaceful morning.

"Be quiet!" hollered Buttercup.

"No, *you* be quiet," Bubbles replied. "I'm playing with bunny."

"Why can't you both be quiet and get ready for school?" Blossom said. Blossom always had to keep an eye on her sisters.

Buttercup was tough. Sometimes she picked on Bubbles for being too girlie. It was up to Blossom as the leader to keep them in order.

"I just don't like how she chatters all the time when she plays," Buttercup complained.

Bubbles continued playing on the floor with her stuffed pink rabbit. "Bunny likes to go hop, hop, hop!" she said sweetly to herself.

A mischievous look crossed Buttercup's face. "Maybe bunny likes to fly," she teased. She grabbed the rabbit and threw it across the room. Like her sisters, Buttercup had superstrength, so the bunny flew superfast and crashed into the hot line. It was a special phone with a direct connection to the Mayor's office.

"Buttercup! Be careful with the

phone," Blossom scolded. "You never know when we may get an important call." She picked up the phone and put it back on its stand. The Mayor used the hot line to call the girls whenever a monster or villain attacked Townsville.

"Yeah," added Bubbles, "what if that mean old Snapper monster came back?"

"Naw, we beat him down good," Buttercup said with certainty. "Besides, the Dragon Bird was much worse. His fire breath was superhot."

Blossom had her own ideas of who was hard to fight. "I thought the Earth King was the grossest. He was sticky and smelly and very mean."

"Yeah, but what about that Blue Beast?" Buttercup reminded her sisters.

"Yeah," Blossom agreed. "He was really awful. His scales were so sharp, it was scary!"

"But they're not the worst," Bubbles whispered.

"Who's the worst, Bubbles?" Blossom asked.

"You know," said Bubbles, afraid to even say the name. She looked around and lowered her voice. *"Him!"*

"Him is the most evil villain of all!" Blossom agreed.

"What's scary is that he can change into anything he wants," Buttercup added. "You never know what he'll look like next."

"Like when he turned into that giant octopus!" Bubbles remembered. "That was awful!" She clung to Blossom's arm.

His ability to change shapes made Him extra dangerous. He was nasty and crafty and mean. Fighting any of those monsters was better than fighting Him.

Chapter 2

Just then the Professor called from downstairs. The Professor had created the Powerpuff Girls in his lab with sugar, spice, and everything nice, plus a dash of Chemical X. Now he was like their dad.

"Time for school, Girls!" the Professor called.

The Girls quickly cleaned up the room and made their bed. Then they flew downstairs.

"Wait!" called Bubbles. "I almost forgot my colored chalk!" She grabbed her chalk from upstairs. Bubbles loved to color on the playground. And she had the best chalk in pretty pastel colors.

The Girls flew over to give the Professor a kiss good-bye. Blossom was first. The Professor gave her a nice pat on the head. Bubbles was second. He tickled her belly, and she giggled as she flew off. Last was Buttercup.

"Play nice," the Professor reminded her gently. Buttercup rolled her eyes and sailed off after the others.

"Have a nice day!" the Professor called out as his Girls flew away.

But the Professor wasn't the only one watching the Girls fly off to school.

"Yes, Girls, have a nice day!" snarled an eerie voice.

Who was it? Only one villain has a voice that scary, that evil. It was none other than Him! Go away, Him, leave the Girls alone.

But Him didn't want to leave Blossom, Bubbles, and Buttercup alone. Him was always looking for a way to break up the Powerpuff Girls. He was all red with mean green eyes. He had a pointy beard, and his hands were lobster claws. He was very, very creepy.

Now Him was watching the Girls from down in his dark lair. He had a special TV screen that showed everything. He could even hear what the Girls were saying as they flew to school.

"Let's hurry, Girls," Blossom said. "I think Ms. Keane is going to review the ABCs today."

"I can't wait for recess," Buttercup said. "I'm going to beat everyone at tag."

"I'm going to draw happy pictures on the playground with my pretty colored chalk," Bubbles added with a smile.

"Coloring is for babies," Buttercup insisted. "You just color sweet, girlie flowers, anyway. Yuck! If I was going to draw a picture, I'd draw mean, scary monsters."

Him's eyes popped open wide. Suddenly he had an idea! Bubbles and Buttercup's bickering gave him the perfect plan to split up the Girls. And if they didn't work together, they'd never be able to stop him. Him cackled with joy as he spun around his dark, creepy lair. This time, he would win!

Chapter 3

The Girls got to school just as the bell rang. Blossom, Bubbles, and Buttercup swooped into the building in time for roll call.

Ms. Keane stood at the front of the class. She was the nicest kindergarten teacher in the whole world. She went around the room calling everybody's name.

"Mary Thompson?" she began.

"Here," Mary answered. Mary was one of Blossom's good friends. They loved to play hopscotch together at recess.

"Elmer? Elmer Sglue?" Ms. Keane called out.

Elmer was busy talking to Buttercup. They'd become good buddies.

"Here, Ms. Keane," Elmer said quietly. He was a shy little boy with dark hair and glasses.

After attendance, Ms. Keane started the lesson. Today they were learning more of their ABCs.

"What word begins with the letter C?" she asked the class.

Bubbles raised her hand right away.

"Yes, Bubbles?" Ms. Keane said.

"Chalk begins with C," Bubbles said proudly.

Then Buttercup raised her hand.

"Ms. Keane! I have another word that starts with C," she called out.

"Yes, Buttercup? What is your word?" asked Ms. Keane.

"Chatter. Chatter begins with *C*," Buttercup said. She shot Bubbles a mean look. "Which is what certain people do all the time."

Bubbles frowned. Then she thought of something. She raised her hand. "Ms. Keane, I know another word that begins with *C*. Coloring!"

Ms. Keane smiled. "Yes, Bubbles. Coloring begins with *C*. I'm not surprised that you thought of that word. After all, you always color such beautiful pictures."

Bubbles smiled up at Ms. Keane. She was the best!

Just then, the recess bell rang. All the kids ran outside. Bubbles grabbed her chalk and flew onto the playground.

chapter 4

The Pokey Oaks playground was shaded by beautiful oak trees. There was a swing set, a sandbox, a jungle gym, a see-saw, and a slide. The pavement of the playground was gray and smooth — perfect for drawing. Bubbles settled down between the slide and the jungle gym with her box of beautiful chalk.

Blossom played hopscotch with Mary. Buttercup was busy playing tag with Elmer around the jungle gym.

As Bubbles colored, she sang and talked about her pictures.

"Coloring, coloring," Bubbles sang. "Coloring a pretty picture. I've got all the pretty colors of the rainbow!"

"I want to draw a flower. Which color is best?" Bubbles asked herself. "Pink! I like pink. And shining on the flower is the happy sun. The happy sun is yellow and orange. All of the happy sunshine also makes the bright green grass grow," she said, grabbing the green chalk.

"And in the green grass lives a little, tiny ladybug. The ladybug is red all over but with little black spots."

"Tag! You're it!" Buttercup shouted over to Elmer.

As she ran away from Elmer, Buttercup skidded right across Bubbles's drawing. Now Bubbles's pictures were all smudged.

"Buttercup, watch where you're going!" cried Bubbles. "You messed my pretty drawing."

Buttercup shouted right back. "Well, if you weren't drawing in the middle of the playground where everyone is playing, it wouldn't get messed up!" She folded her arms.

"Well, if you would watch where you're going, you wouldn't mess up my ladybug," Bubbles replied, standing up and folding *her* arms.

"Who cares about your dopey ladybug?" shouted Buttercup.

Blossom paused in her game of hopscotch. "Bubbles! Buttercup! Stop fighting or I'll tell Ms. Keane!" she called out.

"But —" said Bubbles.

"But —" said Buttercup.

"No buts! There's room enough for everyone. Now play nice!" their sister said.

Buttercup scowled at Bubbles and went back to playing tag. Bubbles knelt back down and tried to fix her picture.

"The pretty flower is growing in the beautiful green grass where the ladybug lives," Bubbles continued. "But then big gray clouds hide the sun away. The clouds drop down lots of nice, wet rain. The rain is blue and shiny. . . ."

"Bubbles, stop talking about the dumb clouds!" Buttercup called out one more time, just to bug her sister.

"Buttercup! Just let her draw." Blossom shook her finger.

This time, Bubbles was too busy to notice Buttercup complaining.

"Raindrops give the ladybug a nice bath and a drink of water. And when the clouds go away, the ladybug is happy and flies around," Bubbles babbled joyfully.

"Bubbles!" Buttercup called, getting angry. "Enough with the sun! Enough with the rain!"

But Bubbles didn't hear a word. She was too happy with her picture. "This is the prettiest drawing I've ever made with the sun shining on my lovely ladybug!"

That was it! Buttercup couldn't stand it anymore. Bubbles's chatter was driving her crazy!

chapter 5

"Be quiet!" Buttercup yelled. She ran over to Bubbles's drawing and smudged it all up with her feet. "I'm sick and tired of hearing you talk about your silly drawing. The ladybug and the flower and the silly sun! Ugh! No more, no more, no more!"

Now Bubbles's flower, grass, sun, and ladybug were just one big mess. Buttercup grabbed Bubbles's chalk.

"Give those back!" Bubbles cried out.

"No way!" Buttercup yelled back.

Buttercup shot supersonic eye beams out of her eyes — straight at Bubbles's chalk. It broke up into a pile of colorful dust.

Bubbles began to cry. Blossom flew over to Buttercup. "That was so mean," she scolded.

"Well . . . she just kept going on and on," Buttercup complained.

"Ms. Keane would be very upset," Blossom said.

"Yes, I would," said a voice the girls knew well. Blossom and Buttercup turned and saw Ms. Keane standing behind them.

"I think you'd better go take a time-out by yourself,

Buttercup," she instructed. "Think about what you just did to your sister."

Buttercup sulked off to a corner of the playground. Blossom started playing hopscotch again.

Ms. Keane walked over to Bubbles and put her hand on her shoulder. "Buttercup is taking a time-out," the teacher told her. "Why don't you bring some more chalk to school tomorrow, Bubbles? Then you can draw another wonderful picture."

Bubbles looked up through her tears at Ms. Keane. "Okay," she said, nodding.

"Maybe you can play with some of the other kids now," Ms. Keane suggested. She patted Bubbles on the shoulder.

But Bubbles didn't feel like playing. She still felt sad. "I just hate it when Buttercup is mean," Bubbles cried to herself.

"But I love it when she's mean," said a

voice. It was a voice that Bubbles couldn't hear. A voice coming from deep down below.

Oh, no! Not Him again! Him, leave Bubbles alone!

Him had watched the entire scene from the special television in his cave. And now he chuckled with glee.

"You may hate it when Buttercup is mean to you, Bubbles. But I love it!" said the spooky villain. "I love how easily you get upset. You're the sweetest of the Powerpuff Girls."

Him watched as Bubbles sat alone by the sandbox. Now was the perfect time to put his plan into action.

"Don't cry, my sweet Bubbles. I'm here to help you. I'll make everything right as rain," Him said with an evil laugh.

Him began to float up from his lair,

heading for the surface. As he rose, he changed shapes. His hair turned gray and his face became wrinkled. His yellow eyes became blue and twinkly. His tall, skinny red body became short and stooped. His tight red suit became a baggy gray one. By the time he reached the top, he didn't look like Him anymore. He looked like a kind, gentle old man.

The old man shuffled his way up to sweet, sad Bubbles as she sat by the sandbox.

chapter 6

"Such a beautiful day, little girl. Why are you so sad?" the old man asked.

Bubbles looked up. She saw the old man looking at her with a friendly smile. She felt silly letting him see her cry.

"I'm all right," she said, wiping away her tears.

"You're not all right. Look at all those tears. Tell me what happened to make that lovely face so unhappy," he said.

Oh, no! Bubbles isn't going to talk to a stranger, is she?

24

But Bubbles was so upset, she forgot this important rule.

"Well," she answered, "I was just sitting by myself, coloring pretty pictures. But then mean old Buttercup ran by and messed up my whole drawing."

"Well, that wasn't very nice, now, was it?" said the old man.

"Nope, it was terrible and mean. And then Buttercup picked up my chalk and shot it with her eye beams and turned it into itty-bitty bits. So now I can't draw at all," Bubbles finished tearfully.

"That is a very sad story," the old man replied, "but it's not the end of the world."

"But now I have no chalk to color with," said Bubbles softly.

"Ah," said the old man, "that is where I can help you."

With that, the old man brought out a small box. Inside was the most beautiful colored chalk Bubbles had ever seen. Each piece seemed to shimmer and shine. Instantly, Bubbles smiled brightly.

"This is very special chalk for a very special girl," the old man told her. "Some people even say this chalk is magic."

"Magic?" repeated Bubbles.

"Yes. Now take this chalk and draw yourself some wonderful pictures," said the man.

No, Bubbles! Don't take the chalk. Never take gifts from a stranger.

Wiping away her tears on the sleeve of her dress, Bubbles gazed into the box. One by one she took the pieces of chalk out. The pieces made a perfect rainbow of colors. Bubbles turned back to thank the old man for this great gift, but he was gone.

Chapter 7

Bubbles looked at her new pretty colored chalk and dove right in.

"This is going to be my best drawing ever!" Bubbles said to herself. "But what should I draw? I'm very good at flowers and ladybugs and butterflies and trees."

But the man had said this chalk was magical. There *had* to be something extra special that she could draw with it. Something different from anything she had ever drawn before.

Then Bubbles remembered Snapper,

the monster she and her sisters had talked about that morning. He was very scary. With these new colors, she could draw that monster better than anyone.

Bubbles drew every detail she remembered of Snapper's body, from his jagged claws to his tough green shell. Even in her drawing, the monster was scary.

"Snapper was a big, nasty turtle monster," Bubbles said out loud. "He had a big belly and sharp claw flippers. He was green all over. He roared through Townsville, crushing every building in his way."

Then Bubbles remembered the other monsters she and her sisters had talked about that morning. She decided to draw them, too. There was the Earth King, made from the dirt and grime of the earth. He grew and grew as he sucked up all the dirt in Townsville.

Then there was the fire-breathing Dragon Bird. He was yellow with a blue belly. He flew above Townsville, setting fire to the city with his flames.

The giant Blue Beast was covered in scales as sharp as needles. He shot his scales all over the city, destroying buildings.

Faster and faster Bubbles drew, coloring every detail of the mean monsters' faces. She drew their fierce pointed claws and razor-sharp teeth. She drew them growling and howling. She was having a great time!

Down in his lair, Him was watching Bubbles on his TV screen. He rubbed his claw-hands together gleefully.

"Oh, Bubbles! You're falling right into my trap," Him said with a grin. "This is perfect!"

Pretty soon Bubbles sat back and looked at her work. These were the scariest drawings she had ever done. Just looking at them scared her!

This new chalk was amazing. Everything looked almost real. In fact, it almost seemed like the monsters were moving.

"That's silly," Bubbles said to herself. "Drawings can't move."

But then Bubbles looked again. The chalk monsters seemed to be shifting slightly. A puff of chalky smoke appeared from the Dragon Bird's mouth. The Earth King seemed to blink one fiery red eye.

Suddenly, the chalk monsters began bubbling up from the ground! With a loud tearing sound, the Snapper's claw burst from the pavement. Bubbles jumped back in shock. The Earth King's red eyes came to life. They shot ray beams right at her!

Terrified, Bubbles darted out of the way. But she backed into something sharp. She whipped around. The Blue Beast's scales were rising from the ground. She felt a tremendous heat as the Dragon Bird's fire breath filled the air.

Bubbles stared at the beasts in shock. Oh, no! The monsters were rising up from the pavement. They were becoming real!

Across the playground, Blossom's superhearing picked up Bubbles's cry.

"Buttercup! Bubbles is in trouble!" Blossom called.

"What's going on?" Buttercup yelled. But before the words were out of her mouth, she found out. Monsters were attacking!

"Bubbles, are you okay?" Blossom shouted. But she could see that Bubbles was in big trouble. The life-size monsters surrounded her, preparing to attack.

34

"Bubbles! Get out of the way!" Butter-cup warned.

But Bubbles just stood there without moving. The monsters were getting closer. Then, just as the Snapper was about to catch Bubbles in his claw, Blos-som swooped in and saved her.

Meanwhile, Ms. Keane had spotted the monsters. "Children, children!" she cried. "Get out of the way!" She rounded up the trembling students and herded them as far away from the monsters as she could get.

The chalk monsters roared angrily. They looked around the playground. The Dragon Bird breathed hot fire straight into the sandbox, scorching every grain of sand black. The Earth King began ripping the grass from the ground. The Snapper ran for the seesaw, crushing it with his claws. The monsters were destroying the playground!

The Powerpuff Girls huddled together for a quick powwow.

"We've got to stop them!" Buttercup cried.

"But how?" Bubbles asked, her voice trembling.

"Wait," Blossom said, thinking. "They look like the monsters we fought before, don't they? But they're different somehow."

"That's because they're . . . they're chalk monsters," Bubbles said between sobs.

"But where did they come from?" Buttercup asked as the Snapper ran by with a pole from the jungle gym in his claws.

"I — I . . . drew them!" Bubbles replied.

"That's impossible, Bubbles," Buttercup snapped. "You don't have any more chalk."

"I do," Bubbles said, shaking. "An old man—he gave me some chalk."

"What man?" asked Blossom. "Where is he now, Bubbles?"

"After he gave me the chalk, he disappeared," Bubbles told her. "I didn't know the chalk would make my drawings come to life." Her big blue eyes filled with tears.

"Guess we know now," replied Blossom.

Just then the girls heard a scream. The Snapper had grabbed Ms. Keane!

"Come on! Let's get him," Buttercup called. She and Blossom flew in to fight.

But Bubbles stayed put.

"What's the matter with you?" asked Buttercup, floating in the air.

Bubbles sat on the ground. "I can't fight them. I made them," she explained sadly.

"Fine," said Buttercup. "You got us into this mess. But I guess we'll have to get us out." She flew off to try to save Ms. Keane.

Bubbles hung her head. She felt terrible about the mess she'd made.

Down in his lair, Him watched happily on TV. He had even prepared some yummy snacks for his favorite program.

"Oh, Powerpuff Girls. How very easy it is to split apart your little threesome," Him said to himself. "And how much fun to cause you trouble! With barely any effort I have managed to get sweet little Bubbles to create the most terrible monsters. This is just too easy. It's almost like child's play!" Him cackled with pleasure.

Meanwhile, the Snapper held Ms. Keane in his monster claws.

"Powerpuff Girls! Help!" she cried.

"This'll be easy," Buttercup said as she flew in. "After all, he's only made of chalk."

"Let's wipe him out!" Blossom agreed.

But as the Girls tried to get close, the Snapper knocked them back.

"He's not weak at all!" Blossom yelled in surprise.

"He's as strong as a real monster," Buttercup agreed. But then she thought of something.

"I have an idea, Blossom. Distract

him!" Buttercup yelled, and flew into the classroom.

Blossom flew around the Snapper really fast, to make him dizzy. Buttercup returned with a chalkboard eraser in each hand.

"Look!" Buttercup shouted to Blossom.

"Great idea, Buttercup!" Blossom yelled.

Buttercup whooshed across the Snapper's arm with the eraser. It worked! His arm smudged and disappeared. It was just as if he were a real chalk drawing.

Without an arm, the Snapper couldn't hold Ms. Keane anymore. The teacher sailed down toward the ground. But Blossom was right there to save her.

"Now let's see how you like fighting with only one claw, chalk monster!" said Buttercup with a sly grin.

But the Snapper was sly, too. With the one arm he had left, he picked up a piece of Bubbles's chalk and drew himself a new claw! The Girls were stunned.

"He's drawing himself back!" cried Buttercup.

"Okay, let's try again. You go for the stomach and I'll go for the legs!" shouted Blossom. "We'll work our way up."

Erasers in hand, the two sisters flew toward the Snapper. They swiped at his belly and his legs. But as fast as they could erase him, the Snapper colored himself back in.

"What good is erasing them if they can draw themselves back?" Buttercup asked.

Before Blossom could answer, they

heard more cries. The other chalk monsters were going after their classmates.

Just then, the Girls heard a cry.

"Powerpuff Girls! Help!" It was Elmer Sglue, the boy who had been playing tag with Buttercup.

The Dragon Bird had grabbed Elmer and Mary in his claws. He took off and started flying away.

"Double laser beam attack!" Blossom called to Buttercup.

Buttercup nodded, a determined expression on her face.

Buttercup and Blossom shot red laser beams out of their eyes at the Dragon Bird. But the Dragon Bird just laughed as the beams bounced off his chalk body. He clapped his wings together, creating a huge cloud of chalk dust.

The dry, chalky dust filled Blossom's

and Buttercup's eyes and throats. They began to cough.

"Blossom, I can't see anything! How are we supposed to fight?" said Buttercup, choking on the chalk.

"Help!" Mary cried. "Blossom! Buttercup!"

"Use your superhearing to guide you!" Blossom called to Buttercup.

She and Buttercup closed their eyes, held their breath, and flew straight into the dust. They could hear Elmer and Mary struggling against the Dragon Bird. With their superhearing turned up to ultrasensitive, the Girls found their classmates and rescued them.

"Raaaaaaar!" screeched the Dragon Bird furiously. It screeched and clapped its wings harder. The chalk cloud grew bigger and bigger. It was too much.

All around the playground, the children ran through the cloud, coughing and choking on the dust. They had no idea where they were going. Some were running right into the chalk monsters!

Girls! You have to find a way to defeat these chalk monsters before they destroy the school. Or, even worse, Townsville!

Meanwhile, Him sat comfortably down in his lair, crunching on his snacks.

"Four chalk monsters against two Powerpuff Girls. This is too perfect!" he said with an evil smile. "I've finally done it. I've come up with the perfect plan to defeat those pesky Powerpuffs!"

Him was so impressed with his own brilliance, he couldn't help but show off a little. With an evil laugh, he rose up from his lair. When he reached the surface, he changed into the old man once again.

Blossom and Buttercup were still busy trying to beat the chalk monsters. But everything they tried had absolutely no effect. They punched. They kicked. They used sonic screams. But the chalk mon-

46

sters were invincible. Any time any of them got hurt, they just redrew themselves with the magic chalk.

Bubbles was still sitting on the ground by the sandbox, crying. The monsters roared, angrily searching for more kids. Blossom and Buttercup were completely worn out. They took a moment to catch their breath. That's when they saw the old man watching them.

"Who are you?" asked Blossom suspiciously.

Bubbles looked up and saw the old man, too. "That's him! That's the old man who gave me the chalk!" she shouted.

"What kind of a game is this, mister?" Buttercup demanded.

"Why, it's my favorite game of all," the old man replied. "A mind game!" He laughed. To the Girls' amazement, he began to transform before their eyes. His suit grew red, his body long and thin. His pointed beard and yellow-green eyes returned. He turned back into their most hated villain!

"Him!" the Girls all shouted together.

Yes! It was Him all the time, Girls! Get Him!

"You were the old man?" Bubbles asked, her blue eyes flashing with anger.

"That's right, Bubbles. I was that sweet old man who cared so much about your troubles. I knew you needed some help, so I did what I could.

48

Wasn't that kind of me?" Him said with a sly grin.

"You! You tricked me!" Bubbles cried.

"Tricked you?" Him asked. "Everything I said was true, Bubbles. That chalk I gave you was beautiful. You *were* able to draw wonderful pictures with it. And it *was* magic. It was just *my* kind of magic. The evil kind."

Now Bubbles was furious. How could she have been dumb enough to fall for one of Him's tricks? But then she thought of something.

"Wait!" Bubbles said, flying in front of Him. "If the chalk you gave me made my drawings come alive, then it wasn't my fault that the monsters attacked. It was really you who made them, not me."

Him was stunned. Bubbles had never gotten so angry before.

"What are you going to do?" Him asked nervously. "You know you can't destroy them. Look what happened to your sisters."

Him was right. She couldn't just destroy them. But then Bubbles smiled. She had another idea.

"I don't have to destroy them. I can fix them!" Bubbles shouted.

chapter 10

Bubbles ran over and picked up the magic chalk.

"What's she doing?" asked Buttercup.

"I have no idea," Blossom replied.

Bubbles flew up to the Snapper with the chalk in her hands.

"Raaaaaar!" screeched the Snapper.

But instead of fighting, Bubbles held up the chalk and started to draw — right on the Snapper's face!

"What are you doing, Bubbles?" Blossom called to her.

"These are mean, nasty chalk monsters. But I can change that. I can make them into happy chalk monsters. That way they'll be nice and won't hurt anybody anymore," Bubbles explained.

"That's not gonna work," Buttercup scoffed.

"Maybe it will," Blossom said hopefully.

"Hmph!" Him sneered. There was no way Bubbles's trick would work. Was there?

Holding her chalk carefully, Bubbles worked on the Snapper's face. She changed his growl to a grin. Instead of snarling, he was now smiling!

Blossom and Buttercup watched closely. Ms. Keane and the kids stood and stared. The other chalk monsters didn't know what would happen.

Bubbles began drawing flowers and rainbows and hearts all over the Snapper's body. Suddenly, the Snapper stopped growling and started giggling happily.

Bubbles raced over to the Blue Beast. Just as he was about to grab her, she started coloring like crazy. She put daisies on all his sharp scales. Then she turned his mean, angry grimace into a loving, happy face. The Blue Beast began to laugh and sing.

"Destroy her!" shouted Him.

"Go, Bubbles, go!" everyone else shouted from the playground.

The Earth King tried to grab the chalk away from Bubbles. The Dragon Bird chased her. But Bubbles raced around, dodging the two remaining chalk monsters at every turn. She was too fast and too nimble for them. Finally, she hid behind a tree.

Exhausted from the chase, the Earth King and the Dragon Bird stopped to catch their breath. They looked around in confusion. They couldn't find Bubbles.

Suddenly, all three Powerpuff Girls jumped out from behind the tree.

"Tag! You're it!" Bubbles shouted triumphantly. "Hold 'em, Girls!"

Blossom held onto the Earth King while Buttercup grabbed the Dragon Bird. Bubbles flew in and gave the monsters happy smiles. Then she covered both monsters' bodies with stars and butterflies. They changed from the meanest monsters to the sweetest monsters ever. The Earth King and the Dragon Bird joined the other chalk monsters laughing and dancing around the playground.

"Great job, Bubbles! You did it!" called Buttercup.

"No!" screamed Him in pain. "No!"

Him was furious. How did Bubbles do this? His plan was perfect. Everything had been going so well. But Bubbles wasn't finished. Just as Him thought things couldn't get any worse, she flew up to Him with the chalk in her hands.

"You think that's bad?" Bubbles asked with a gleam in her eye. "Watch this!"

Shooting her eye beams, Bubbles broke the magic chalk into a pile of dust, just like Buttercup had done to her chalk earlier that day. Him crumpled to the ground, defeated.

"Just you wait, Powerpuff Girls. When you least expect me, I will return," Him hollered as he oozed back into the ground.

chapter 11

Bubbles heard cheering. She turned and saw her classmates from Pokey Oaks jumping up and down. Blossom and Buttercup flew to congratulate her.

"Smart thinking, Bubbles," Blossom said.

"Yeah, that was really awesome how you got Him all chalked up," Buttercup agreed.

"You did a great job." Ms. Keane smiled.

"Yeah!" shouted all her classmates.

"Thanks, everybody. I'm just sorry I made such a mess," said Bubbles.

"Well, if I hadn't been acting so mean, then Him would have never given you that rotten chalk," Buttercup replied. She hugged her sister. "I'm sorry."

"That's okay. Besides, look at the happy monsters we have as our new friends," Bubbles said.

The Girls watched as the nice, friendly chalk monsters helped the children and Ms. Keane clean up the Pokey Oaks playground and fix the equipment. Now the chalk monsters were using their super-monster powers for good instead of bad.

Once everything was fixed, the chalk monsters played with the children. The Snapper gave them rides on his back. The Dragon Bird flew them in the air. The Earth King played with them in the mud.

And the Blue Beast let them slide down his scales. Bubbles was happy that everything was all better.

Oh, Bubbles! Look how you've drawn us all together!

And so, once again, the day is saved, thanks to the Powerpuff Girls!